This magical
Barbie Annual 2007
Belongs to:

_____

Aged:

_____

Also known as:

Princess
_____

Fairy
_____

EGMONT
We bring stories to life

Published in Great Britain in 2006
by Egmont UK Limited
239 Kensington High Street,
London, W8 6SA.
Printed in Italy

ISBN 978 1 4052 2610 3
ISBN 1 4052 2610 2
1 3 5 7 9 10 8 6 4 2

Written by Jane Clempner
Designed by Sheryl Bone

Close your eyes tightly.

Now imagine a land far, far away, at the end of the rainbow ...

An enchanted place where flowers sparkle like diamonds

and colourful butterflies dance on the breeze ...

There's more than one side to every
Barbie girl ... as you are about to discover! x

In this magical land, pretty flower fairies flutter and play ...

Count the number of peonies - the big
pink flowers - that you can see.

And fairy dust
falls like rain …

Welcome to Fairytopia!

My name is Elina and this is my home.
Fairytopia is the happiest place you could
ever imagine; I love living here! During the day,
I dance and play with my friends, the flower fairies.
We play hide-and-seek in the flowers of the
Magical Meadow …
And when we are tired, our friends the butterflies
take us home …

Colour in the letters in Elina's name.

Elina

Which colours can you see
in the butterflies' wings?

At night, I sleep in the soft, scented petals of a Lotus Flower ...

Around my neck, I wear a necklace
with magic powers. It helps me keep
Fairytopia safe. The powers were given
to me by the wise Enchantress.
I only use them against bad fairies
who want to take our beautiful land
for themselves ...

Point to Elina's magic necklace.
What two colours can you see?

Every day is a magical day in Fairytopia.

Colour in Elina, using the picture opposite to help you.

No two butterflies in Fairytopia are the same!

Can you colour in these butterflies so that they are all different?

There is only one Elina, though!
Draw a line to match Elina to her shadow.

a.

b.

c.

d.

Flower Power!

It was another beautiful day in Fairytopia.

Elina was in the Magical Meadow collecting fairy dust for her friend, Dandelion.

During a game of Catch, poor Dandelion had fallen off her butterfly and broken her wing!

"Dandelion's wing will soon be as good as new," said Elina, scooping the magic dust into her silk purse. "I've never seen so many flowers in the Magical Meadow! All must be well in Fairytopia!"

But Elina spoke the words too soon. For, at that moment, the sky turned black and three of the wickedest fairies in any kingdom appeared on the hill.

The ugliest of the three called down:

"Hurry home and pack your bags, fair Elina. Fairytopia belongs to us!"

"Never!" said Elina. "Not as long as I have my magic necklace …" She lifted her hand to touch the necklace and gasped. "My necklace … it's gone!"

"Exactly!" cackled the second fairy. "And without it you are powerless to stop us!"

"Why won't you leave us alone?" pleaded Elina.

"Because we want your Magical Meadow!" said the third. "Look how many flowers there are this year."

"All the more for us to pick and boil for our spells!" said the first.
"We'll give you until midnight to leave ..." And they flew, laughing,
to the ugly black cloud that was darkening the sky over Fairytopia.

Elina sat down and began to cry.

A crystal teardrop rolled down her cheek and landed on the ground.
In an instant, every flower in the meadow closed its petals and all their
colours drained away. Then a pathway appeared.

Elina jumped to her feet and followed the path. It led her to the only
flower still in bloom. And there, lying safely in its pink petals, was her
magic necklace!

Quickly, Elina put it on. "It must have slipped off when I was playing Catch," she said. "I would never have found it without your help …"

Suddenly, the flowers all opened their petals and the meadow filled with colour once more.

In the sky, the black cloud drifted away, taking the wicked fairies with it. And the sun shone again over Fairytopia …

With a sprinkling of fairy dust, Dandelion's wing was soon better. And Elina gave up playing Catch, for at least the rest of the day!

The End

Fairytopia is safe as long as Elina wears her magic necklace.
Show her which path to take to find it.

a.

b.

c.

Fairies need their wings to fly! Draw some pretty wings on Elina's friends to help them fly.

Flower Power Game!

Put the colour back into the Magic Meadow! Play with a friend. You will need a dice and some pens or crayons. Take it in turns to roll the dice.

Player 1

The number that you roll is the number of flowers that you may colour. The winner is the person who colours in all the flowers in her meadow first.

Player 2

Make Magic Happen!

Now you can make magical butterflies, just like the ones in Fairytopia.
All you need is some paper, paints and coloured pens.

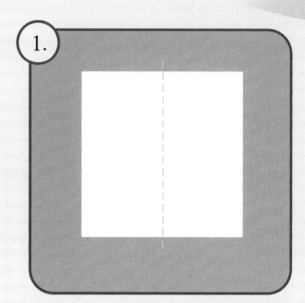

1.

2.

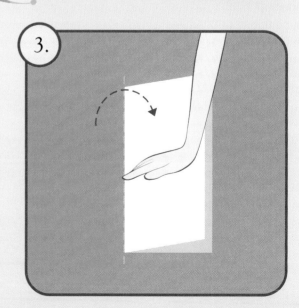

3.

Note to Parents: Adult supervision is recommended when sharp-pointed items such as scissors are in use.

1. Fold your piece of paper in half.

2. Open it out and paint a pattern on one half of the paper only.

3. Fold your paper in half again and press down lightly.

4. Now unfold the paper and hey, presto! You have made a butterfly as magical as any in Fairytopia!

5. When it is dry, add some details with your coloured pens.

Now put up your picture for everyone to see. Why not make lots of butterflies – no two will ever be the same!

The flowers in Fairytopia are very beautiful!

Can you copy each flower into the grid opposite, one square at a time?

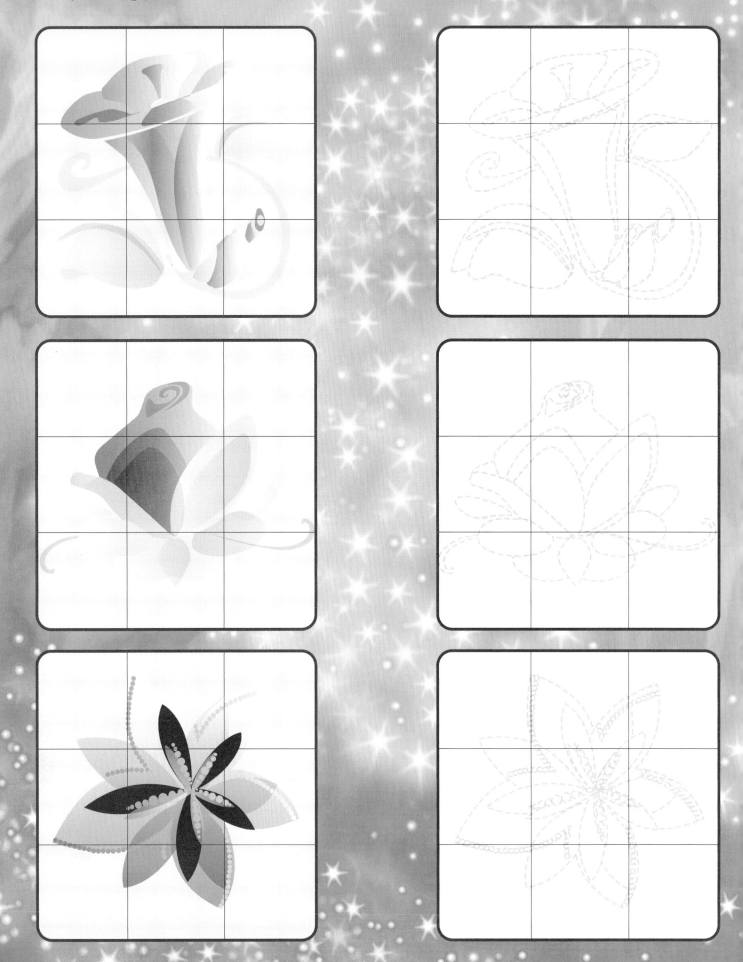

5 flower fairies are playing hide-and-seek in the Magical Meadow!
Can you find them all?

At night Elina sleeps in the petals of a Lotus Flower.

There are 6 differences between the two pictures.

Can you find them all!

Colour in a petal for each difference you find.

In Fairytopia, magic fairy dust falls like rain!
Join the dots in the stars to see something magical appear!

The flower fairies are as pretty as flowers! At night they curl up inside a flower that matches the colour of their wings. Draw lines to match the fairies and their flowers.

a.

2.

1.

c.

b.

d.

3.

4.

Elina is searching for her missing necklace. Colour in the picture using your crayons or pens.

Elina has found her necklace! Colour in the picture to show that all is well in Fairytopia.

Goodbye …

I hope you have enjoyed
your trip to Fairytopia.
Whenever you want to
visit again, just close your
eyes and let your imagination
take you …

Say goodbye to Fairytopia, but remember, there's more than one side to
every girl and there's more than one side to this annual!
Come back soon, Elina x

I've been thinking about all the things I love!

I love to doodle and I love to dream

I love things that make the world a prettier place

I love being a girl because we have so much fun

I love dressing up and changing my look

I love being a princess one day, and a tomboy the next

I love being with friends, and making new ones

I guess I just love being Barbie

Remember, there's more than one side to every girl and there's more than one side to this year's annual! So check out the other side! Bye for now,
Love Barbie XXX

Later that day, Lola knocked at Uncle Greg's door, carrying a colourful box. "I've brought my beads," she said, as Barbie welcomed her in. "I thought we could make bracelets."

"Not until I've painted your nails!" replied Barbie.

And from that moment, the girls were inseparable. Some days they went diving and snorkelled. Other days, they lay in the shade swapping secrets and dreams. Lola remembered how beautiful her island was. And Barbie had the best holiday ever.

All too soon, it was over.

"Next holiday you're coming to stay with me!" said Barbie, as the taxi arrived to take her to the airport. "I'll show you my town!"

"Try and stop me!" smiled Lola. Then she added, "Things are so much nicer when you have someone to share them with …"

Barbie gave her a hug. "A friend makes all the difference …"

Lola laughed: "A bit like nail varnish!"

Nail Varnish and New Friends

Barbie was staying with her Uncle Greg, who just so happens to live on a Caribbean island!

"Totally dreamy!" said Barbie, stepping on to the white beach on the first morning. She sunbathed and swam. She wrote postcards and swam some more. But, by the end of the day, she was bored!

"Why don't you go exploring?" suggested her uncle, who was busily opening his beach café the next morning. "Take the bus …"

The nearest town was only a mile away. Barbie decided to walk.

She set off along the dusty road. There was a girl standing at the bus stop. She was tall, with dark hair, and she wore lots of colourful jewellery. Barbie thought she was beautiful.

"Is this the bus stop for town?" asked Barbie.

"Town?" laughed the girl. "I wouldn't really call it that!"

"Do you live here?" asked Barbie.

"Worse luck," said the girl. "I can tell by your clothes that you don't!"

"I love your necklace …" smiled Barbie.

"And I love your shoes, your top and especially your nail varnish. I could never find that colour here!"

"My uncle's house is right there," said Barbie. "Why don't you come over later, if you're not busy?"

The bus arrived.

"Thanks!" said the girl, climbing aboard. "I'm Lola, by the way …"

Now read my picture postcard to find out what I did on my last holiday.

Hello, from  !

It's so beautiful here. The  sing in the

and colourful  swim in the sea.

Every day, I sit under my  and fan myself

with a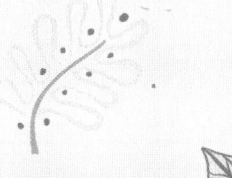

I'm eating lots of 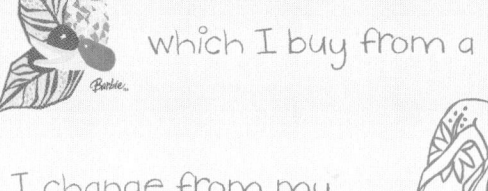 which I buy from a

. At night, I change from my

to my  and put on my  .

Then I head for the 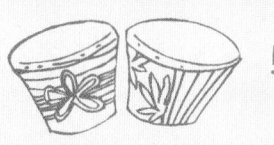 club and samba

to the rhythm of the !

Wish you were here!

Love Barbie XX

When it's cold outside, the best way to warm up is by looking at your holiday snaps! Colour in this picture of my friends and me last summer.

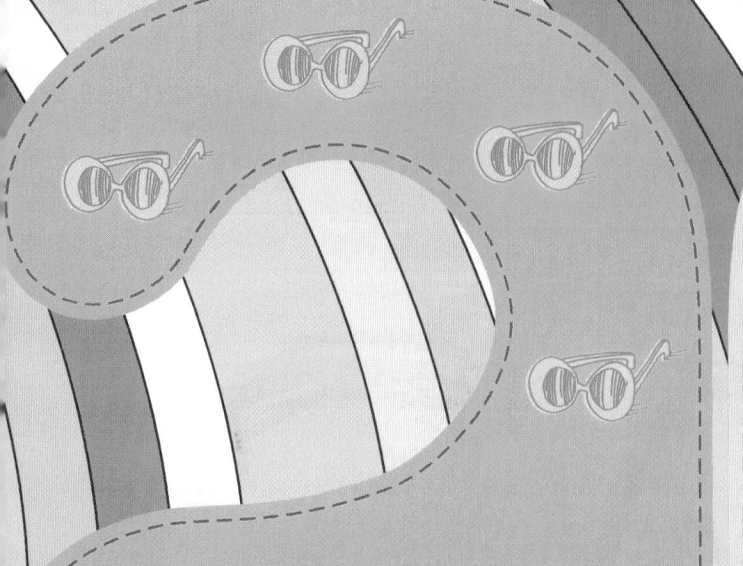

KNOCK IF YOU ROCK!

_____

Fill in your name.

LIKES HER MUSIC LOUD!!

Shhhhhh!! Princess

_____

Fill in your name.

needs her beauty sleep.

A rock chick likes company, but a princess needs her privacy!

There are two sides to every Barbie girl!

Make a double-sided door hanger for your bedroom door, just like the one Barbie has.

Turn it over to suit your mood!

You will need:

- Scissors
- A piece of card
- Glue
- Coloured pens

Scissor alert – ask a grown-up to help you with the cutting out.

What to do:

1. Write your name in the spaces on both sides of the door hanger using coloured pens.

2. Ask a grown-up to help you cut the door hanger from the page.

3. Cut a piece of card to the same size and shape as the door hanger.

4. Glue the two sides of your door hanger to opposite sides of your piece of card.

Now your door hanger is ready for action!

The Pink Dolls are my favourite band.
I like them so much I have two copies of all their CDs - one for
my bedroom and one for my car!

Can you match the CDs into pairs?
Circle the odd one out!

My bedroom walls are covered with posters! I don't let many people in, but you can take a peek here!

Colour in the butterfly next to the poster you like best.

The music festival was cool. But the next time I went out for the evening I made sure I looked my best!

Here, Barbie and Teresa are wearing their best evening outfits. Colour them

I bought two copies of this poster from the music festival, but when I got them home, I found there were 6 differences between them. Can you spot them?

Colour in a guitar for each difference you find.

5 Which kind of shop are you happiest in?

 A clothes shop

 A pet shop

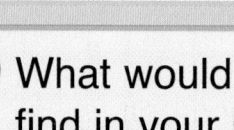 A toy shop

6 What would you most like to find in your Christmas stocking?

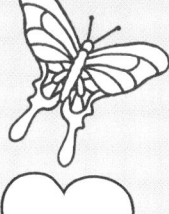 Sparkly jewellery

 New trainers

 Pens and crayons

7 Where would you most like to listen to music?

 Lying in a bubble bath

 At a live music festival

 In your bedroom

Mostly butterflies ...

You are a butterfly waiting to spread her wings! You're a real girly girl who loves to look pretty and dress up and dance, like me! But remember, you don't need a tiara to feel like a princess!

Mostly hearts ...

You are a girl who is as kind as she is beautiful. You are caring and thoughtful and adore animals, like me! You don't need frills. You're a tracksuit and trainers kind of girl.

Mostly flowers ...

You like to look pretty, but you're also happy in your scruffs! You can't quite decide, just like me! Luckily, you look good whatever you wear!

Take this fun test to see if you are a tracksuit or tiara kind of girl!

Answer each question truthfully! Colour in either the butterfly, heart or flower next to your answer. At the end, count which one you have coloured most.

1 Which colour do you wear most?

- Pink
- Green
- Blue

2 What do you like best about going to a birthday party?

- Shopping for a new dress
- Playing party games
- Blowing out the candles and making a wish

3 What do you like to do at the weekend?

- Go to a dance class
- Ride or walk in the country
- Watch TV or play

4 Which fairy-tale character would you most like to be?

- Sleeping Beauty
- Snow White
- Cinderella

Oh, no! It's started to rain!
I have my keys, but where did I park the car?

Show Barbie the way back to her car, but avoid the lightning strikes along the way!

I gave them a hug, "I love you guys too! But please let me go and change!"

I ran back inside and pulled on my most comfortable combats and a pink top. I hid my hair under a cap and with a touch of lip gloss, I was ready.

I grabbed my car keys and off we went. We played the latest Pink Dolls CD all the way there. It was the coolest gig ever and that day made me realise how brilliant it is to be a girl!

And two weeks later I found out I'd passed the exam with Honours!

"Here we are," said Mrs Greenburgh as we pulled up at my house. Then she looked me up and down. "You should run inside and change!"

I rushed upstairs and scattered kirby grips over my bedroom floor! Then I turned my head upside down and shook the rest of them out. I caught sight of myself in the mirror – I looked like a scarecrow under a haystack!

Downstairs my cat was meowing to go out, so I opened the front door. "W – what are you doing here?" I gasped. My front garden was full of my friends!

"Did you forget the music festival?" laughed Teresa. "We're ready to go!"

"Interesting outfit!" smiled Kira. "Luckily, we love you whatever you wear!"

It's a Girl Thing

Being a girl means that you can be glamorous one day and a tomboy the next!

Ballet exams are not one of my favourite things! I do love wearing a tutu and having new ribbons on my shoes, but I don't like the hour you have to spend getting ready! Mrs Greenburgh, my dance teacher, puts my hair in a bun with at least fifty kirby grips! Ouch! They hurt! And then she sprays it into place with a giant can of hair spray!

"A dancer must suffer to look beautiful …" she said, moments before my last exam.

I tried to smile, then the music began and in I went …

Fifteen minutes later, it was all over. I was hot, tired and my hair hurt!

"I will take you home, Barbie," said Mrs Greenburgh. "But please hurry …"

There was no time to take off my tights, so I slipped on my sandals and pulled my tracksuit over my tutu. I did look odd!

Next, I straightened my hair and tried out a sporty summer look. Do you like it?

And here I am striking a pose! The layered look is really in. We made a pretend catwalk and practised our walks and turns! Modelling is great fun!

Why don't you try a home fashion shoot with your friends? It's so much fun!

Last weekend, I invited Teresa over for a home fashion shoot! I have a cool new camera and we wore our latest outfits and tried out some new looks ...

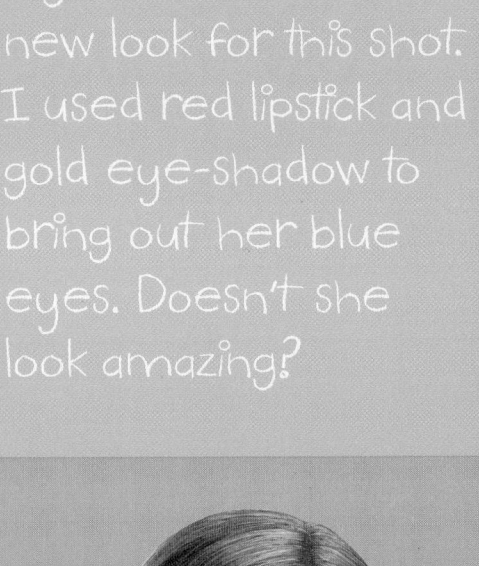

I gave Teresa a whole new look for this shot. I used red lipstick and gold eye-shadow to bring out her blue eyes. Doesn't she look amazing?

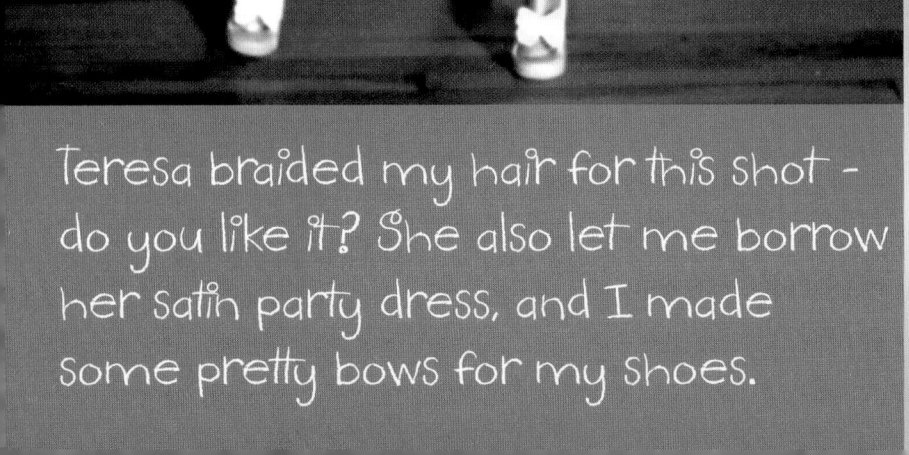

Teresa braided my hair for this shot – do you like it? She also let me borrow her satin party dress, and I made some pretty bows for my shoes.

Being in the wild-flower garden made me want to draw!

Colour in my drawing using your crayons or pens.

She led them into the garden shop and stood in front of a display of seed packets. "Look, Kira," she said. "If you plant wild flowers in your garden they will attract insects of all kinds. By the summer you'll have a real live collection that will grow every year. Much better than silly shoes!"

Kira smiled. "Thanks, Barbie, you're the best friend anyone could ever have!"

And the wild-flower garden soon became the most magical place in Barbie Town.

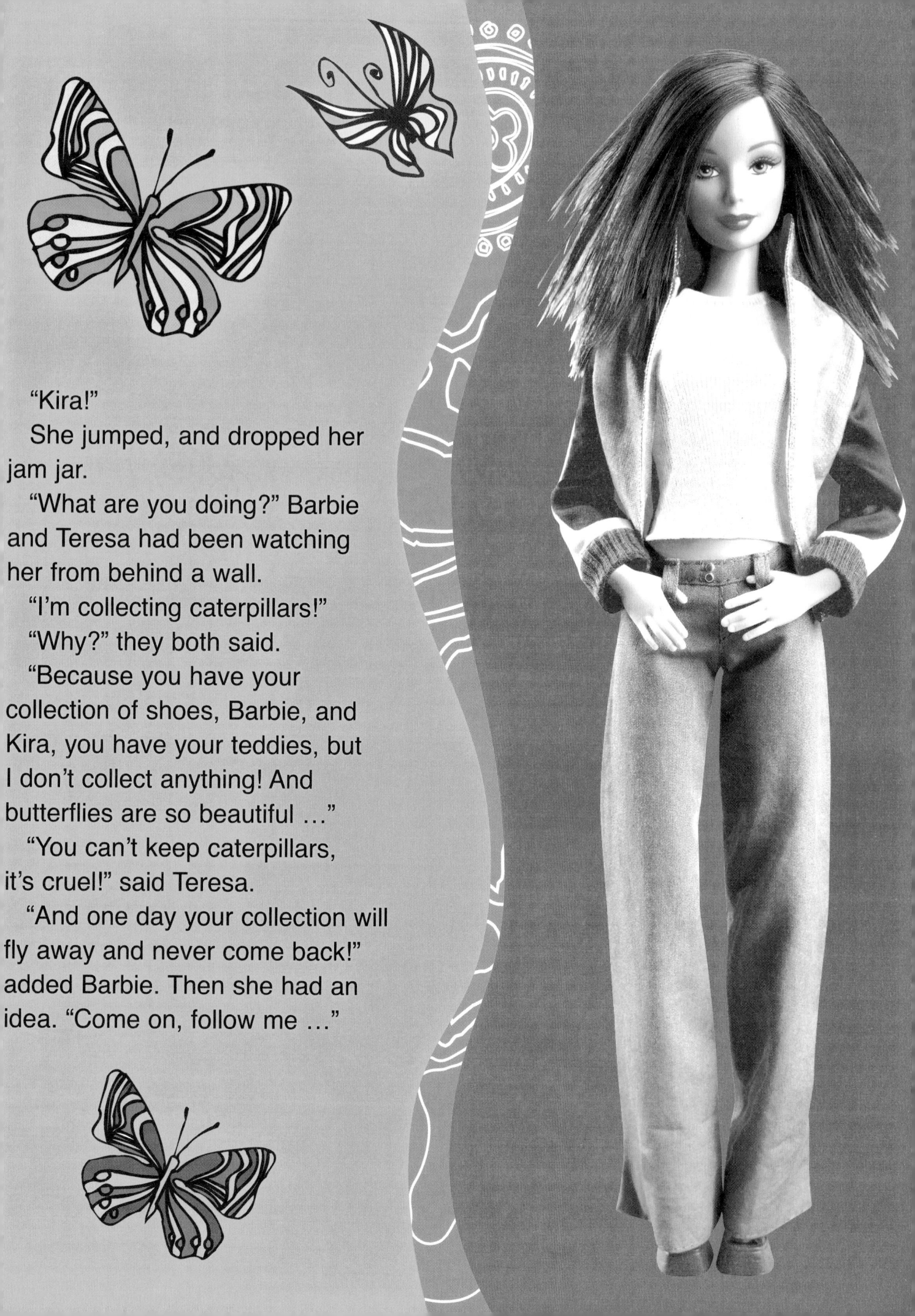

"Kira!"

She jumped, and dropped her jam jar.

"What are you doing?" Barbie and Teresa had been watching her from behind a wall.

"I'm collecting caterpillars!"

"Why?" they both said.

"Because you have your collection of shoes, Barbie, and Kira, you have your teddies, but I don't collect anything! And butterflies are so beautiful …"

"You can't keep caterpillars, it's cruel!" said Teresa.

"And one day your collection will fly away and never come back!" added Barbie. Then she had an idea. "Come on, follow me …"

Chasing Butterflies

It was a sunny Saturday in summer. Barbie, Teresa and Kira were sitting in the park.

"Shall we go into town later?" suggested Barbie. "There's a new shoe shop opening ..."

"But there's a Teddy Bear Fair at Hale House," said Teresa.

Barbie turned to Kira. "Which would you rather do?" she asked.

Kira shrugged. "I'm not really bothered."

"Is something wrong?" asked Barbie.

Kira was about to reply when a beautiful butterfly landed on the bench. The girls watched it until it flew away.

"Actually, let's go to Hale House," said Kira, a smile lighting up her face. "There's a garden there ... Meet you at the entrance in twenty minutes ..."

The sun was still shining as the three girls arrived at Hale House. Kira waited until Barbie and Teresa were inside then slipped away into the gardens. From her bag, she pulled a jam jar. Then she started to creep along the bushes. "Now," she whispered, "to start my collection ..."

We're girls on a mission!

Colour in Barbie and Teresa on their shopping trip, using your crayons or pens.

Barbie girls love to shop!

Can you find two shadows that are exactly the same?

Answer: Shadows a and e are the same.

Teresa, Kira and I love to visit our favourite department store. With five floors of fashion, we can be there all day!

Last time we went, Kira brought her new puppy along for the ride …

Just being in this store makes me feel like a princess. Who needs a red carpet when you can have pink fluffy ones?

So many gorgeous shoes and hats just waiting to be tried on for size!

Well, I found the perfect present for Teresa – a pink bag to go with her new outfit …

And, as it was nearly Christmas, I treated myself to a handbag and shoes to go with my new coat …

Barbie's fashion trail

I love shopping – especially with my friends. We always like to look our best …

Teresa found just what she was looking for – a pink party outfit. It was divine …

Then I spotted this amazing coat with fluffy cuffs. I just had to have it!

We moved up a floor to the shoe department. Now, this is my idea of heaven …

I've been good all year, I think I deserve it!

Barbie
X

4 Make sure you always smell sweet!

3 Walk tall and straight – good posture makes all the difference!

2 Give yourself a treat every day – you deserve it!

1 Always, always, always wear something pink!

Remember, you don't need lots of $ to look like a ♛!

The secret to feeling like a princess, is learning to spoil yourself! So here are my top ten tips on looking and feeling like a true princess ...

10 When shopping, carry lots of bags, even if they're empty!

9 Look your best at all times!

8 If you do have to be practical, stay pretty!

7 Try to match your bag with your shoes!

6 Always carry sunglasses, even in winter!

5 Look out for posh labels – even if they're fake!

What's *fab* about being YOU?

Make a list of the things YOU love to do!

I love to ... _____

_____

_____

_____

_____

There are 5 roses on this page.
When you find them, colour them your favourite colour!

Being Barbie is *fab*! There are so many gorgeous girly things to do! I love to ... go shopping! And try on new clothes ... I love to play with make-up! And listen to music ... I love to collect shoes! And chill with my friends ... I love wearing things that sparkle! Especially if they're pink!

There are 5 sparkly rings on this page. When you find them, colour them pink!

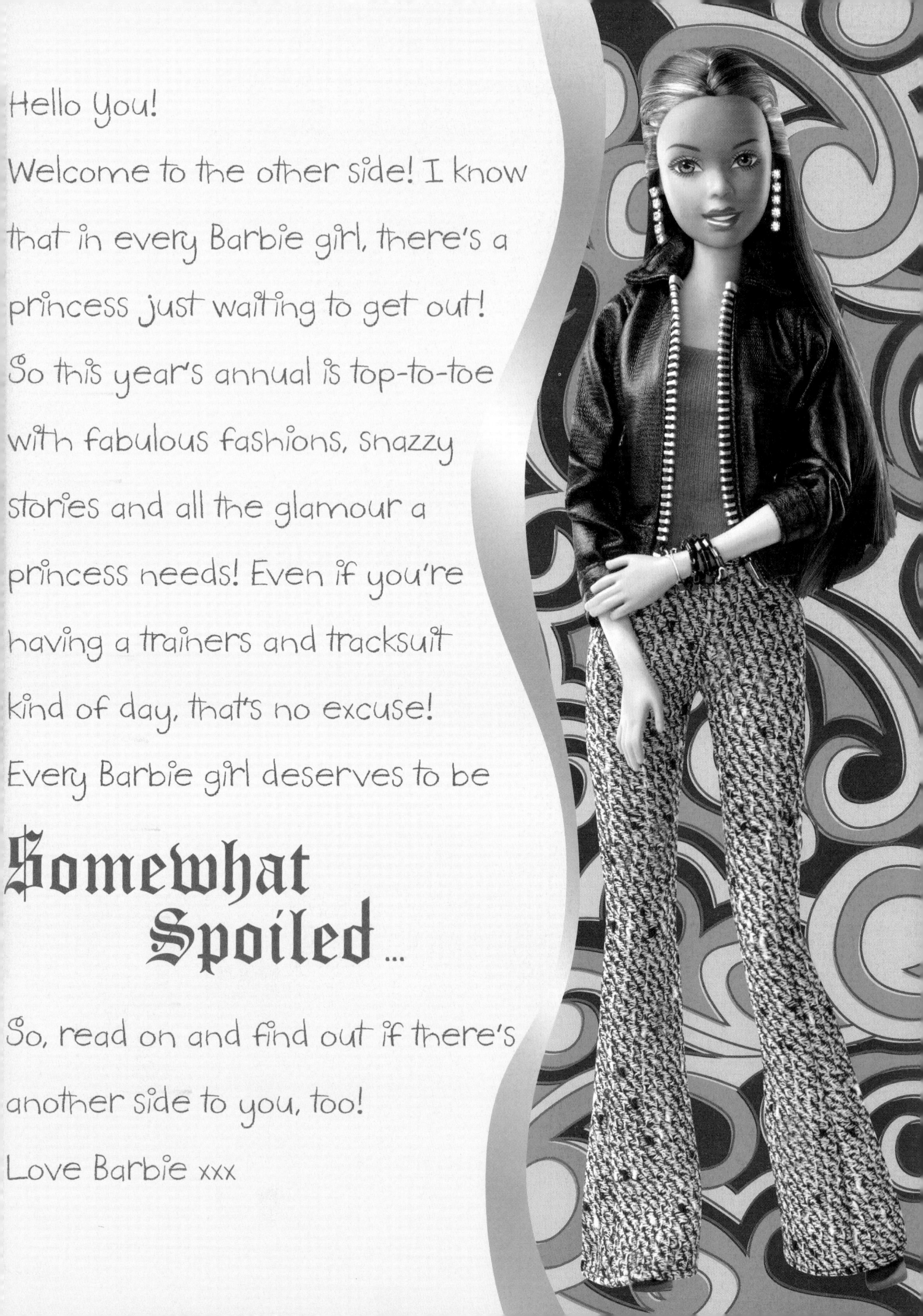

Hello You!

Welcome to the other side! I know that in every Barbie girl, there's a princess just waiting to get out! So this year's annual is top-to-toe with fabulous fashions, snazzy stories and all the glamour a princess needs! Even if you're having a trainers and tracksuit kind of day, that's no excuse! Every Barbie girl deserves to be

Somewhat Spoiled ...

So, read on and find out if there's another side to you, too!

Love Barbie xxx